SYX
WHOLE
WEEKS

SITUATIONSHIPS
BOOK FOUR

GREYHUFFINGTON

Copyright 2024 © Grey Huffington
All rights reserved.

The content of this book must not be reproduced, duplicated or shared in any manner without written permission/consent of the author except for the use of brief quotations or samples in a book review, blog, podcast, or social media post without harmful or infringement intent.

In other words, if you're looking for inspiration, don't draw it from this book or any book that you read in the Grey Huffington realm. I employ you to dig into your brain and find something suitable to write and for your audience to read. My creativity is precious and duplication (of any manner) is inconsiderate, repulsive, highly offensive, and dead-ass wrong. Please move around.

In the event that this work of fiction contains similarities to real locations, people, events, or situations, it is unintentional unless otherwise expressed by the author.

instagram.com/greyhuffington

LET'S GET SOCIAL

Instagram:

Grey Huffington
(Cover reveals, releases, etc)
Instagram.com/greyhuffington

HuffingtonHQ
(News, updates, etc —headed by Team Huffington)
Instagram.com/huffingtonhq

TikTok:

Grey Huffington
(Vlogs, updates, promotional images/videos, etc — headed by Team Huffington)
TikTok.com/@greyhuffington.com

Pinterest:

Grey Huffington
(Inspiration, quotes, snippets, visuals, boards, lifestyle, etc —headed by Team Huffington)
https://pin.it/695pEOV9m

TRIGGER WARNING

PLEASE READ THIS SECTION!

Seeing this note means the book you are about to read could contain triggering situations or actions. This book is subject to one or more of the triggers listed below.

**Please note that this a universal trigger warning page that is included in Grey Huffington books and is not specified for any particular set of characters, book, couple, etc.
This book does not contain all the warnings listed. It is simply a way to warn you that this particular book contains things/a thing that may be triggering for some.**

This is my way of recognizing the reality and

life experiences of my Romance friends and making sure I properly prepare you for what is to unfold within the pages of this book.

violence
sexual assault
drug addiction
suicide
homicide
miscarriage/child loss
child abuse
emotional abuse
mental illness
infidelity
infertility
cancer
criminal activity

NOTE.

Between the covers of this book is **my** art piece —beautifully paired words structured for **my** creative satisfaction and later consumed by others for enjoyment.

It's leisure for you, it's **life for me**. This is just a book to most. **It's art for me**. *My* art. I've had *my* time. Have **yours**.

happy reading

CONTENTS

Syx Whole Weeks — xiii

1. Syx — 1
2. Trough — 7
3. Syx — 13
4. Syx — 23
5. Trough — 29
6. Syx — 37
7. Syx — 43

ghuffington.com — 51
More from Grey Huffington — 53

ONE
SYX

NEW YEAR WAS JUST around the corner and Trough was adamant about celebrating our second year anniversary. However, I was a bit hesitant for the second year in a row due to the circumstances under which our union was formed. I'd much rather celebrate the day that I'd accepted him back into my life as our anniversary, but that didn't seem to matter much to Mr. Mallard.

It was our first kiss that he wanted to replicate. It was our first moment of intimacy that he was desperate to celebrate. According to him, he'd known that we'd one day be in the position that we're in now. His ex-wife only had a matter of time before her shit came crumbling down, and it had done just that. He'd waited, patiently, for our time to come and it was as beautiful as he'd imagined.

Considering the position that we were in at

the moment, I wondered if he'd actually known that we'd be side by side, his right leg tucked in between both of mine as I stared at him through the darkness dreading the trip to the bathroom that I'd been needing to take for the last ten minutes. Insomnia had become my worst enemy. For the life of me, I couldn't get a full night's rest without waking up wondering. It was the strangest knowing that these types of nights were few and far apart. The only time I was confined to my sleepless cell that I called a bed was when Trough was away on business and the warmth of his body wasn't attainable.

But, here he was. Sound asleep as I gazed at his honey colored skin with a shriveled face that produced worry lines across my forehead. Closing my eyes, I sighed knowing that I'd have to get up at some point to relieve my bladder because there was no way I would get comfortable with the ache that had formed on my side. Tucking my tail underneath me, figuratively, I tossed the bit of cover that Trough was nice enough to loan me through the night from around my body. Pushing forward, I wasn't surprised to feel his grip around my waist tighten as Trough pulled me in the opposite direction. At the slightest notion of me leaving his side, his restraints doubled.

"Where are you going?" He groaned from the comfort of his pillow.

"The only place there is to go at four in the

morning, Trough. I have to pee," I chuckled lowly, noticing the conversation we were currently enthralled in was agonizingly repetitive as well as pleasurable.

Attachment on any level displayed by Trough Mallard was appreciated. Though I wasn't the woman who required a man's attention to breathe, I appreciated every bit that I received from my man. Contentment was my other enemy, no matter what the situation was. I was a strong believer in continuing the chase even after you'd made the catch and Trough hadn't failed me yet. I'd stopped running long ago, yet he was relentless in his chase. Not only had he caught me and captured my heart, but he'd secured me for life according to the rock on my finger that required daily exercise to maintain without tearing a muscle.

A heavy sigh followed my response, assuring me that my fiancé approved my trip to the bathroom. My heart galloped in my chest as the beats per minute increased. I could feel the indentions in my cheek sink as my lips curved upward to form a smile. Before tossing my legs over the bed and scooting from his grasp that had been loosened, I cupped the side of his face and placed my lips over his.

With the difference in size, they covered half his chin and nearly touched his nose. I could feel the slight adjustment to his breathing as he opened up and allowed my tongue inside.

The silence of the night was once again interrupted, but this time it wasn't by words. It was the smacking of our lips and wrestling of our tongues that caused a ruckus. My heart ached as we tore away from one another, making my trip even more regrettable. As much as Trough wanted me beside him, I wanted to be. The cold, lonely bathroom was the last place I wanted to be for the next few minutes while I handled my business.

"I'll be right back."

My words weren't only for soothing Trough, but my raging heart as well. One foot before the other, I tipped towards the bathroom in a pair of fuzzy socks. I was thankful I hadn't managed to take them off during the course of the night because I'd need the cushion to protect me from the cold marble I was seconds away from stepping onto.

Inside of the bathroom, I passed up the light switch. There was a small plug in illuminating the shiny, hard surfaces and leading the path that I walked to access the toilet. My teddy was up and ass was being lowered in a moment's notice. I could feel small prickles all over my body as I avoided perfect posture and allowed my back to hunch and shoulders to slum.

"Ummmm," a moan evaded me.

After my bladder was emptied, I patted my pussy dry with the thick tissue that had come from the dispenser beside the sink. Then, I removed a wipe from the warmer on the back of the toilet to remove any remnants of urine that was left behind. This step was crucial with the knowledge that Trough had no reservations when it came to intimacy. In the middle of the night he'd wake me with his head between my legs. At the crack of dawn, I'd find him nibbling away at my clit. To save him the trouble of licking through the saltiness of my flesh due to my mid-morning bathroom runs, I cleared it with the wipes we had handy.

My return to the covers we fought for each night was gratifying. I slid underneath them as Trough maneuvered in bed to accommodate me. He'd rolled over onto his stomach during my brief absence. The human cocoon, he lifted an arm – raising the cover – and held it in place until I was snuggled against his body. Each groove of his matched each curve of mine, completing our two-piece puzzle.

When I was comfortable, his arm fell over my body and was stuffed underneath the side that was flat on the mattress. Back in his grasp, Trough pulled me in even closer before resting his face between my shoulder and chin. Insomnia was no longer an issue as the rhythm of his breathing lulled me to sleep as a nursery rhyme would a newborn.

TWO
TROUGH

IT WAS the most gratifying sensation in the world. Sliding into *my* Syx each morning and breaking her off a dose of the dick that was available exclusively to her. I didn't have to lie to myself anymore like the pole that I had just casted to fish in her pond was mine. Simply put, my dick didn't belong to me. It was *hers*. Hers to touch. Hers to suck. Hers to ride. Hers to keep. Hers to care for and baby girl never disappointed.

My eyes connected with the back of my skull as I touched rock bottom. Syx squirmed in front of me, wiggling as if there was any more room left to fill. She'd been dead to the world when I cocked her leg, slightly, and slid inside of her. Forever moist, I had no issues breaking through her barrier and finding my way home. I didn't care how repetitive morning sex was for us, each morning it felt as if we were embarking on new territory.

"Who's pussy is this?" She moaned.

There was this significance to Syx. Many men would consider it a complex, but I thoroughly enjoyed every bit of it. She wasn't the average. The type of woman to submit to a man each and every day of her existence. Syx preferred spontaneity. Most days I was demanding of her from what she wore down to what position I wanted her sucking my dick in. Then, there were moments like the one currently presented to us where she utilized my vulnerability to her advantage. And, frankly, I was always vulnerable when it came to the pussy. *Her* pussy to be specific.

"Mine," I whimpered into her thick, curly mane.

"Who's?"

Syx had no intention of playing fair this morning. I could hear it in her tone and gauge just how erratic she was planning to be by the sudden movements she was administering in front of me. Both of her hands gripped the side of the bed. She was searching for a stable foundation to accommodate her. Once she was in position, she pushed into me.

"Mine," I managed as she pulled away from me, almost removing me completely from her pussy before pushing back against me, again.

My toes locked, popping as I curled them

as far as my bones would allow. Syx was tossing that ass of hers back with one goal in mind. *Unmanning me this morning.* Without a doubt, she would succeed, but I'd had plans for her little ass. This wasn't a part of them, but I wouldn't complain. Her audacity was commendable and there hadn't been a ride she'd taken me on that I didn't return overly satisfied and burned the hell out.

"Shit, baby," I was forced to grab her waist in an effort to control her movements. My attempt failed miserably as I felt the familiar sting of her small hand.

SMACK!

"Let me go, Trough," she demanded, pushing my hand from her frame after she'd assaulted me.

"Baby," I pleaded with her.

"Roll over," was her response.

"Syx," I tried, again.

"Roll over, Trough," she gritted.

Still inside of her, I rolled up both over until my back was flat on the bed. I was extremely apprehensive about the new position we were in. It was one I avoided as often as possible, knowing I wouldn't last. Couldn't last. Not with all that ass slamming into me, the sight of Syx's massive curls bouncing on her head and witnessing her creaminess slathered on my dick each time she raised up.

My eyes closed involuntarily as I felt her

cuff my ankles with her hands for stability. She began to rotate her hips in a circular motion before rising and falling onto my shaft. Over and over, she repeated the same movement. Each time she raised up, I was afraid to see what more of a mess she'd made between us but couldn't smother my curiosity for the life of me. I found myself with my eyes wide and neck straining from lifting off the pillow beneath me to see my baby get down for me. Thick strands of creamy goodness stuck to her ass every time she rose, connecting us still. Syx made it to the tip of my dick with each lift, giving my head the attention she thought it deserved. Mission not yet accomplished, Syx upped the ante by reaching forward and grabbing my sack. She massaged my balls with her fingers and kept them centered in the palm of her hand. I nearly ran my ass up the wall when I heard the sound of her saliva being extracted from her mouth and onto my shit.

SPPPT.

A glob of spit landed on my sack, lubricating it in addition to her juices. My head fell backward onto the pillow behind me. I wasn't any good. My lids lowered as my peak neared. I could feel the nut being extorted from my balls, traveling up my shaft, slowly.

"I'm bout to cum, baby," I announced so low that I didn't think Syx would hear me, but I was absolutely incorrect.

Swiftly, she slid off my dick and replaced her pussy with those big lips of hers. I had no time to decline or no choice in the matter when I felt her lower lips on mine and the warmth of her mouth claiming it's hostage. Syx's head bobbed, slicing the air as she tried to suck the skin from my dick. I fell in line, planting my entire face in her pussy. I needed to bring her to her climax, even if it meant her cumming after me.

THREE
SYX

"OH, SYX!" Sevyn's voice crooned through the speaker.

"Opening up," I responded, pressing the button that allowed me to talk to her from inside.

There was a zapping noise before the handle of our door was pulled open. In waltzed Sevyn with bright eyes and a bushy tail. She'd gotten a few blonde highlights over the summer and they were beginning to fade. However, they stood out like sore thumbs against her deep, dark chocolate skin. Her natural curls were full of life, following her lead.

"Good morning," she cheered, sitting two cups of green tea on the counter as we made it to the kitchen and removing her coat before sitting on the stool.

"I'm guessing Ace gave you some dick this

morning?" I toyed, seeing as though she was extremely hyped.

"Ace gives me dick almost every morning. But... this morning... he licked this pussy from the rooter to the tooter. THEN, he gave me some dick. See, there's the difference," she clarified.

"Yeah, I can see it all over your face," I leaned forward and pretended to examine her face with scrunched eyes.

"Get the fuck out of my face crazy ass girl. I brought you some tea over. It is freezing out there."

"Per usual," I reached for the cup holder and grabbed one of the teas. "Come on. Let's head next door. I want to show you this piece I've been working on."

"For who?"

"An artist of Trough's."

"That nigga stay putting you on, Syx. I really hope you're sucking that man's dick every night as a natural sleep enhancer," Sevyn gave me a serious face to let me know that she was not joking.

"I sucked his dick this morning as a matter of fact. So, no. Not always at night. Most times when he makes it in, I'm already asleep. Now, can you quit inquiring about my sex life."

"Wait, didn't you just ask me if my nigga gave me some dick this morning? But, I can't ask if you're breaking your man off properly?

Whew, chile. The nerve," she twisted her neck and rolled her eyes.

Chuckling, I responded, "Okay. You have a point. But, still. You're all open about yours. I try to keep mine on the low."

"Because you want to continue being a little closet freak. I've pulled your card too many times to know that you aren't as innocent as those curls and curious eyes make you look."

"Screw you!"

"Na. Screw Trough. I'm getting dicked down enough these days."

I led the way to my studio, which was only a few feet away. Trough had purchased two amazingly beautiful homes that were side by side. One was much smaller than the other, which was perfect for its purpose. We'd transformed the home into a design studio with the first floor serving as a showroom and fitting area. Upstairs is where the magic happened. There were four rooms upstairs.

One was my office and the other three were occupied with projects I had started or intended to. I never worked on more than one piece at a time. Each required a different headspace and mood, so I separated them and visited often until they were completed. It was my goal to finish them all around the same time so that I could clear out each of the rooms and start fresh every three to four weeks.

"See what I'm saying!"

"Well, you set yourself up for that one. Please put a move on it. I left my coat next door and you're taking too long to turn that key!" Sevyn fussed from behind.

She'd been correct. It was freezing out and neither of us had grabbed our coats because the design studio was so close. Picking up the pace, I disabled the two locks that kept my work safe and let us into the heated studio. Each time I walked in, I was amazed at the fact that every single piece of it belonged to me. Trough was more than generous with his donation.

Up the stairs and into my labs, I led Sevyn so that she could check out the pieces I was constructing. They were so beautiful, though simple to construct. The colors were bold and the fabric was pleasurable to work with.

"Damn," she belted as we walked into the third design room, "Who running up a check like this?"

"That singer... Harlem Knight. According to Trough he's caking on someone he's been having his eye on for a while. You've probably heard of her, too. Sleigh Wellington."

"Who hasn't heard of her? She's goals for all of the little brown ballerinas of our time."

"Well, I got some tickets to her show, courtesy of Harlem Knight."

"They're together, together? I thought he was single." Sevyn admired the red tutu. It was my favorite, next to the brown and olive-colored pieces.

"For now. He's on a mission to steal this one's heart."

"Obviously! I love a man who's all about the chase! This nigga isn't playing any games," Sevyn howled.

"He ordered fifteen of them."

"You've got to be shitting me. How much are you charging per piece?"

"Twenty-three hundred dollars."

"Girl. I'm in the wrong business. Fifteen for twenty-three hundred dollars?"

"I'm making the shoes to match. Each one will have matching flats."

"Get out of here!" Sevyn's eyes bulged from her sockets.

"No. Seriously. The shoes are one thousand a pop. They're custom with her initials monogrammed on the strings," I assured her.

"Thirty-three hundred dollars per fit and there's fifteen of them? Ace has to step his game up!"

"Don't even try it. Are you not forgetting that Ace is in the market for you two a home? He's gotten you a car that you don't even drive because you'd prefer for him to pay for you to be driven around? What about the vacations? The celebrations? The random gifts that he just keeps on giving? Example, that damn ice sculpture on your wrist he just got you two months ago?" I reminded her, quickly.

"You kind of have a point there," Sevyn piped down. "Anyway, what was so important that you called me over so early in the morning? I had to get up with Ace just to make sure I got up at all."

"I know. That is why I specified the time, knowing that he and Trough would be working together this morning."

"That still doesn't answer my question," Sevyn removed a freshly rolled blunt from the pocket of the sweater she'd been wearing underneath her coat. It was dazzling, to say the least. The mustard yellow was complimenting her melanin. "We going next door any time soon? I brought us a little pick me up to get our day started."

"Yes. We're leaving now," I responded with a nod.

Smoking in the studio was prohibited. There was even a special place in our home that was dedicated to my guilty pleasure so that the entire house wouldn't smell like the goodness that the earth had managed to create. Within three minutes flat, we were inside my home, again. Before Sevyn was able to make her way upstairs to the private area, I pulled her towards my cell that was laying on the kitchen counter.

"This is why I called you over. I've been

scared shitless. I needed to know that I'm not tripping."

I scrolled through my applications and landed on the period app that I'd used religiously for years. Sevyn utilized the same one, so there were no questions asked when I opened it and showed her what I'd been seeing for the last week. There was a leery silence lurking, which encouraged the uneasiness that was already present in my body. As the seconds grew to a minute, I became undone as I waited for my outspoken sister to finally speak.

"Nine days," she let out with a shallow sigh.

"And counting," I added.

"You're nine days late. Syx. You're never late!"

This was a fact that we both were aware of. I couldn't remember a single time that my period had run circles around me or came unexpectedly. If anything, I'd come on my period a day early and that was because of the differences in days in each month. But, late... never. I wasn't even sure how to feel not seeing blood at least ten days prior.

"And Trough is fixed," I reminded Sevyn.

"See. You're jumping to conclusions. I've been late all my life, so my period is always falling in line," she chuckled, attempting to make light of the situation, but I would sense the uncertainty in her tone.

"No. I'm not, Sevyn. I've had insomnia for a minute now. I'm up at all hours of the night peeing. I've had a lack of appetite, only able to keep down certain foods. I won't even start on the fatigue I've been feeling lately. I'm exhausted beyond belief and we both know that isn't like me. Thankfully, I have a set turnaround time for any piece I make. It is the only thing that is saving me on my current project. Those tutus are pretty simple compared to other things that I make, but I find myself asleep on the sofa downstairs more than I'm upstairs tending to them," I confessed in one breath, so happy to finally get everything off my chest. I'd been holding it all in for at least a week.

"Oh. Damn," Sevyn's eyes bulged as she sat her tea on the counter. "I guess I should just put this away, huh?" She asked, referring to the blunt in her hand.

"Yeah. That won't be happening any time soon."

"So, you really think you're pregnant?"

"I don't see how, other than the fact that my man can't have children. He's going to assume I am cheating, Sevyn! He has gone through this once with his ex-wife."

"And you're not her. Yes, it may seem impossible, but something isn't adding up."

"That's probably exactly what he will be thinking," I took a seat at the counter.

"Didn't he say he ended up getting a blood test on that little baby to be certain there wasn't a chance it could be his?" She inquired.

"Yeah," I recalled.

"Okay, then. There you have it. He must've been told that there was a possibility that this could actually happen. You guys have been fucking like wild animals for two years, now. He's been nutting all in that thang. Let's just face the facts, Syx. One of his little soldiers was determined enough to see it's way to the end of the tunnel," Sevyn shrugged as if she'd just solved a trigonometry equation.

"Obviously!" I agreed. "But, there will be doubts, Sevyn. I know there will be."

"That damn man knows that you aren't cheating on him. We all know. Now, before you go stressing my little person in there, let's make sure that this little person even exists. Where is the nearest pharmacy? I'm going to have my driver to go pick up a few tests," Sevyn offered.

"No need. I bought a few boxes the last time I was out. I've been waiting to take them."

"And you're just calling me over?"

"I haven't wanted to face the facts. Guessing and knowing are two different things, Sevyn. Come on. We're going to use the bathroom downstairs."

FOUR
SYX

"PREGNANT?" I questioned as if it was my first time seeing the results.

In fact, it was the third time the word had appeared across the small glass window as I stared down at the stick I'd pissed on. Two days ago my sister and I had huddled in the bathroom to read the results of my first test. Confirming my suspicions, the word appeared on the screen and nearly sent me into cardiac arrest.

Still in complete disbelief, I'd come into the bathroom each morning after and soiled another stick with my urine while silently praying for different results. It wasn't that I was apprehensive about pregnancy or having a child. However, the circumstances didn't exactly permit the happiness that I was supposed to be feeling at the moment. Instead, my thoughts were clouded with fears of rejection and confrontation. Those were the last things I wanted right now.

"Baby!" Trough's voice boomed, causing me to drop the stick that I held with the tips of my fingers.

"Shit," I fussed and fumbled to retrieve the test from the floor.

"Why you got the door locked?" He questioned, calming my galloping heart in my chest.

I thought surely I'd forgotten and he was about to walk in. Holding my chest, I cleared my throat and spoke up, "I don't know. Out of habit, I guess. One second."

Leaning forward, I flushed the toilet that was in the downstairs guest bath. I took advantage of the loud swooshing of the water and other sounds to conceal my actions. Once the test was secured under the cabinet with the rest of them, I unlocked the door. Trough was standing outside of it waiting with curious eyes.

"You just left. What are you doing back so soon?" I was a nervous wreck, pumping soap into my hand before starting the water at the sink.

"I want to take you to breakfast. I've been up and out of here every day this week. When I come home, you're knocked out."

"Sounds like somebody is missing somebody," I teased, my cheeks aching from the blushing I was doing.

"I am. Now, get your ass out here so we can

go woman. You're going to scrub the black off your hands. Trust me. They're clean, baby," he chuckled.

I hadn't noticed I was still hovering over the sink washing my hands. "Right!"

"I'm going to be waiting for you in the foyer. Don't be long, Syx. I have a schedule to keep."

"Did you come back home just to rush me? If so, we can stay in and I could cook something. You'll be back out of the door and headed to work in less than an hour."

"I'm not going back to work. I've cancelled my dealings for the day," he informed me.

When Trough felt that I was being neglected in any way, everything stopped. Life in general for him was put on hold until he was satisfied with my pampering. It wasn't enough to send flowers, pay for massages or sponsor shopping sprees. Trough preferred his presence over his monetary gifts and I appreciated that about him. He knew that he couldn't buy me and he'd never tried, either.

"And, you're not lifting a finger to cook this morning. I can pay people for that. I'd prefer for you to relax with me. Tomorrow is the New Year and I need to make sure you have everything you need."

"Trough, you're really serious about this whole anniversary thing, aren't you?"

"When have you ever known me to bluff,

Syx? If it falls from my lips, then it is set in stone. A man's word is all he has. If he doesn't have that, then he doesn't have himself shit."

Shaking my head, I dried my hands with the towel on the drying rack and followed him through the hallway. "Alright. I'll be back down in a few. I promise not to keep you waiting long."

The truth was, Trough would've waited forever if he had to, but I wouldn't make him. I valued his time as he did mine. There was a mutual respect there that was unspoken but abided by at all costs. When I was returned to his side minutes later, we headed for the door.

FIVE
TROUGH

IT WAS her choice this morning. I wanted whatever she was having in addition to some of her time. Seemingly, I'd been separated from Syx for the last few weeks with so much going on with business. Oftentimes, I felt as if I was neglecting the home-front to make sure that business was in order, but the minute I caught myself slipping I'd regroup. That's exactly what had happened this morning on my way into the office. Syx was on my mind something awful.

We'd been carrying on as we usually do, sex in the morning with her pussy for breakfast, but I could feel a wedge being lodged between us. Even now, we were so close but she felt miles away. Ever so often, I'd catch her drifting away. I wondered where her mind would wander to, but knew that there was no reason to pry. She'd tell me whatever was on it when she was ready.

The waitress appeared jarring us both from our thoughts.

"She will have a mimosa and I'll have an orange juice to start," I responded to the waitress's question.

Snapping into reality, Syx quickly readjusted the order to suit her desires this morning. "In fact, let's cancel the mimosa and go with a glass of apple juice instead."

"Be right back," the waitress nodded.

"I was on the toilet this morning. I'm not sure a mimosa will do me any good," Syx chuckled, slightly.

"Na. You chose the right thing. Do we need to stop and get you something after we leave?"

"No. I'll be fine. I think Sevyn passed her bug on to me. She's just getting over a stomach bug and was over the other day. I knew I should've disinfected. I..."

"You looked beautiful this morning," I interrupted, noticing she'd begun to babble. Something was definitely on her mind and I wanted to help put her at ease. "Bug or not."

"Thank you," her head lowered as she soaked up the compliment I had just given.

"No thanks was necessary," I reclined slightly in the chair I was seated in. "So, how are those fifteen pieces coming along?"

It was important to know what Syx had going on in her world. The last thing I wanted to be was clueless and seem careless when it came to her dealings. Each time I was able, I sent new clients her way. She was making her way to the top and I couldn't be prouder. The studio that had been created for her next door was a winner. She hated venturing too far and preferred a home-like atmosphere over a work environment. It was perfect.

"They're coming along. Fairly easy, but I'm enjoying seeing my designs come to life, per usual. I can't wait until they're all completed and shipped. They're beautiful."

"I can believe it. I'm going to come take a look at them this evening when we make it back home. A few of the fellas are tying the knot soon. I've been getting requests for your contact information left and right. They've passed the information along to their fiancés. Be on the lookout for strange area codes calling. They're all from Channing."

"Will do. I truly appreciate the business you send my way. It makes me feel like I'm not getting out enough to bring in more clientele myself," Syx admitted. She'd always felt this way, but I didn't mind putting money in her pockets.

"You're fine where you are. You have the entire Instagram thing going for you. Let's not act as if that isn't bringing in mounds of clientele. I've seen your schedule for the next few months. I didn't send all of those people to you, baby. Take some credit here."

"You're right. I do pull in a lot of business from social media. Mostly because I'm always getting tagged by the clients who I service. Every time that happens, I get a heap of new followers."

"That leads to even more clients."

"Right, but the largest jobs usually come from..."

"Shhhhhhh," I placed a finger to my mouth to stop her in her tracks.

"Here you are. Are you two ready to order?" The waitress placed our drinks on the table.

"Yes. As a matter of fact, we are."

My eyes never left Syx's gorgeous face as I placed an order for us both. She could barely sit still under my gaze, squirming in her seat with a smile plastered on her face. Everything about her made the cavities of my chest stretch to capacity as my heart swelled twice its size. Two years in and I was in much deeper than when we'd started. That was putting it lightly. My investments were so plentiful with Syx and she deserved every bit of them. My time. My money. My effort. My love. My heart. My dick. It was just as much hers as it was mine.

. . .

OUR FOOD WAS DELIVERED SHORTLY after our order was placed. Conversation continued to flow as we poked at one another, asking the questions and making the statements time hadn't allotted in the last few weeks. It was always delightful catching up with baby girl. It wasn't until I noticed she hadn't eaten much of her food that I drew concern.

"In the mood for something else?" Her chicken and waffles were basically untouched.

"No. I'm just scared to put anything on my stomach," she sighed, placing her fork on her plate and giving me those eyes. There was a longing within them that I tried pinpointing, but she tore them away from me before I was able.

"Understood," I replied and continued to fork my food. "At least hydrate yourself. Let me get you another apple juice."

"Okay."

Laughter was plentiful during the course of our meal. It was rewarding to see her in such a festive mood. Plans that I made for the following day came to mind and I knew that we'd better get a move on it if I was going to make sure everything was handled in time. Syx still needed something to wear, because I'd noticed she hadn't shown off anything new she'd made for herself in a while. That meant she was still on the fence about exactly what she would dress as well as the celebration in general. However, I wasn't concerned much with her hesitation. It was our official anniversary and we would celebrate it as such. New Year had become my favorite holiday for that reason alone.

"We have a full schedule. We should get going."

SIX
SYX

HAIR.
Nails.
Fittings.
Jewelry.

It was all extremely nauseating to think about. It was well into the evening when I decided I simply couldn't hang any longer. It was time to break the news to Trough and I couldn't wait a minute longer. I felt as if I was about to puke my guts out and then fall out shortly after. It was imperative that I be taken back to our home to rest and possibly grab a few hours of sleep.

"Trough, baby. I can't go any further," I belted in the silent enclosure we were in viewing the lovely necklaces that had been laid out in front of me to choose from. "I need to get home."

"What's the matter?" Trough asked, laying

the necklace he was inspecting beside the others and turning towards me.

"I'm not sure. I just don't feel so well."

I could feel my health declining as I whined. Trough pulled me closer until my head was resting on his chest. He, then, lifted a hand and laid it on my forehead. I figured he was checking for a temp, but I didn't have an elevated one. Closing my eyes, I enjoyed the softness of his skin pressed against mine.

"You feel fine. What's hurting you? What's the matter?"

"I feel queasy. Pretty soon I'll be puking up the little food I got down. I may even have to do number two," I whispered. It was crucial that I continued the façade that I'd started at breakfast.

"Do you see anything here you like? Just pick one and I'll have it ready by tomorrow," he waved her other hand over the black velvet cases.

"I can't choose. I like them all, baby. Maybe you can choose for me."

"I can't either. Ahmad." Trough stood and grabbed my hand for me to follow him into the front of the store. "I'm going to take them all. Neither of us can decide. Send me the tab and have them ready in the morning. Someone will be by to pick them up."

"Sure thing, man," Ahmad nodded as we headed for the door.

"Trough. Wait. I can choose. We don't have to get them all. That is at least seven!"

"One for each day of the week. Sounds ideal to me."

"Where do I even go to need seven, baby?"

"Doesn't matter. I want you to have them so you'll have them. Get inside of the car so that I can get you home," he demanded as he opened the back door.

Obliging, I slid into the car and waited for him to follow suit. "I can't believe you."

"Believe it, baby. I'm going to pour you some ginger ale. Maybe this will help settle that stomach of yours." Trough leaned over and began fumbling with the mini fridge that held a few bottles of wine and liquor as well as liquids to mix them with.

We reached the inside of our cozy nest just in time for me to make a beeline for the downstairs bathroom before I ruined my clothes. The puke that had been threatening to spill over had finally made good on its promise. On the floor, I clinched the sides of the toilet as my apple juice, the ginger ale I'd been given and small fragments of waffles and chicken filled the bowl beneath me.

"Damn," I heard Trough mumble just before I felt his large hands pulling my thick curls backward.

There was fumbling on the counter before my hair was stretched even further. When I saw both of his hands as he made his way to the floor where I was I realized he'd put my hair into a messy bun. I'd taught him the simple hack after he complained about not being able to see when I was sucking his dick. My hair was almost always in the way of things.

"Shit," I groaned once I felt like I'd emptied everything that I could. "Baby, can you go get my toothbrush and toothpaste? My mouth feels yucky."

"Yeah. Hang tight."

Trough rushed off upstairs as I tried getting myself together. He returned shortly after and watched as I brushed my teeth at the sink. When I was done, he helped me clean up a bit and then lifted me over his shoulders to take me up the stairs. Maybe it was obvious that I wouldn't be any good if I tried tackling them myself. My energy had been depleted.

I fell into the bed once we made it upstairs. Removing my shoes and clothes wasn't an option, because I didn't have the strength to do any of them. I was thankful for Trough's help as I watched him remove my boots and lay them on the floor beside the bed. After they were off, he pulled my shirt over the ponytail he'd made and then moved on to my pants.

"You want everything off?" he questioned.

"Please," I nodded.

My underwear was next. Trough tossed them in the clothing basket right along with the other articles he's removed. Too hot to get underneath the covers and too cold to remain on top of them, I requested a blanket from the closet, instead. Trough removed his clothes and shoes before climbing in bed and pulling me upward until my head was on his lap. He activated the television and began watching the sports channel while running his hands through my scalp. I didn't recall falling asleep, but I drifted into a deep slumber at some point.

SEVEN
SYX

I COULD FEEL his eyes burning holes in my skin. My own darted towards the digital clock on the wall and noted that it was after ten at night. I'd slept the entire day away, but I felt rejuvenated. The rest I'd gotten was necessary. There was a glimmer of light coming from the television, which helped me to see a bit better. Trough was hunched over the chair he'd brought into the room waiting for me to make eye contact with him.

"Hey," I got out, still trying to wake.

There was silence before Trough responded. I knew that whatever was about to come out of his mouth I probably wouldn't like. When he went cold on me it usually meant that something was wrong or something had happened. My stomach knotted and a lump formed in my throat.

"Are you able to get up?" He inquired.

"Yes. Is everything okay?" I tossed the blanket from my body and lifted from the bed.

He didn't respond this time. Instead, he stared at the bottom of the bed where my feet had been. My eyes followed his and my heart leaped into my throat once I noticed what he was staring at. Three pregnancy tests were lined up on the bed. They had all been used and were all familiar.

"Why didn't you tell me?" His voice raised a notch. I couldn't discern if he was angry, heartbroken or frustrated at the moment. There was one thing I knew though and it was that he wasn't happy.

"I- I don't know. I just found out a few days ago and I've been terrified ever since," I admitted.

"Of what?"

"I don't know. I guess you being mad at me like you are, now."

"I'm not mad at you, Syx. My pride is a little bruised. I'm a little hurt. Shit like this, you're supposed to be running to me with. I know the reason that you haven't is because of the baggage I once carried around."

"You can't have kids, Trough."

"The chances are slim to none, Syx. Nothing is one hundred percent except sustaining and I haven't been able to do that since the first time I slid into your shit."

"I just thought that you would think I was cheating."

"There isn't much I don't know about you, Syx, and I know damn well you aren't cheating. The thought has never even crossed my mind. That- that's what is fucking with me. The fact that you let that stop you from telling me that we're going to have a baby. This isn't something I'd ever want you to try and hide from me. I wish you could've ran through the house screaming this shit to the top of your lungs because you felt that free... that comfortable and that happy. Does this make you happy, Syx?" He lifted the stick.

The pain in his eyes was evident, now. They were glossed as if there was a possibility of misting and maybe even a droplet. I wasn't counting on it, though. Trough was Trough. Tough as they came. I was reminded of the question he'd asked as he moved from the chair to the bed. Taking a moment, I considered my feelings or the lack thereof and decided to be honest.

"I haven't taken the time to really embrace the news because I've been too worried about what you may think."

"I fucking knew it, too."

Trough jumped from the bed and began pacing the floor. I watched as he came unglued. His brown skin was fire engine red as he turned back to me and dropped to his knees.

"Don't ever let the mistakes of the next bitch cloud your judgment or steal your moment. You're nothing like her and our situation is completely different. I know this ain't what you want to hear, but I barely pulled my pants down for her. I can't keep them up when I'm with you. If ever you mentioned children, I had my doctor on standby to reverse this shit. But, life has a funny way of doing things. The universe is on your side even when you don't know it."

"Are you happy? Does this make you happy?"

"Happy? Baby, I can't explain how this makes me feel. I'm not even ashamed to admit that I shed a few when I went under the bathroom cabinet to find the cleaning products and found these instead. I just want to make sure you feel the same way."

A smile emerged and the weight I'd been carrying around was lifted, "I think I'm happy, too."

"I hope you are, because ain't no turning back, now. You're stuck with me for eternity. Eighteen years is just the starting point," he responded, leaning forward and kissing my lips. "Now, put some clothes on because there is someone here to see you."

"Who?"

"I hired a midwife."

"Trough. You just found out while I was asleep."

"And I hit up my partner Kierce. He and his wife, Reign, remember her?"

"Yes. Of course."

"They have two young ones and suggested this midwife. I called in an emergency and we've both been waiting for you to wake up. I hope you don't mind, but Ace and Sevyn are on their way over, too. I decided to celebrate the new year at the house since you're not at your best."

"Are you sure you're celebrating the new year or do you have a new reason, now?" I chuckled, calling his bluff.

"Alright. I'll admit that I called Ace over to pop a bottle and light a cigar. It's a new motherfucking Mallard on the way that is worth celebrating tonight."

He was too hype for my comfort, bobbing his head and scrunching his face. This wasn't the poised man I'd grown to love but he'd due. "Oh, Lord."

"Come on. Get up, momma. Let's see what is going on in that belly of yours!"

TROUGH REMAINED at my side through the entire exam. True to his word, he'd hired a midwife. I could already see that he'd be a handful during this pregnancy. According to him, my only job was to carry the baby and get it to him safely. He'd handle the rest. I begged the difference, but you never knew with him. Trough was unpredictable. By the time I made it downstairs and sent Tamara, the midwife, out of the door, I could smell cigar smoke and hear the corks being popped on bottles.

"This nigga done finally scored one in the hole! Congratulations, cuz!" I heard Ace howling.

Shaking my head, I closed the door behind her and prepared for the craziness that was about to go down. We were minutes away from the countdown and I was suddenly feeling festive. After all the worrying I'd done, things had panned out to be just fine. With Trough, I should've known, but you could never be too certain. Ever.

Right along with me, I found Sevyn at the counter shaking her head and laughing at the theatrics as well. I plopped down in the seat next to her and let out a sigh. The cat was finally out of the bag and I felt like I could finally breathe again. Sevyn turned to me almost immediately and wrapped her arms around my neck. We fell into conversation as I ran down my visit with the midwife to her.

"So, how far along are you?" Sevyn reached out to touch my invisible bump.

"Six whole weeks," I responded, catching Trough's gaze.

The smile on his face was priceless. I couldn't say that I'd ever seen him glowing as much as he was at the moment. Our little miracle had quickly become the source of celebration, stealing the New Year and anniversary hype. Or, so I thought. As the television screen blanked and the countdown appeared, my fiancé stood and straightened his posture. Slowly, he took one step at a time and I thought that my heart would burst from the anticipation. By the time he reached me, I was near cardiac arrest.

"Three. Two. One," he whispered in my ear. "Happy Anniversary and Happy New Year. You've given me the best gift a woman can ever give a man besides her love. I love you."

Sevyn ventured off, wrapping her arms around Ace as I felt Trough's hand rest on my stomach. His nose brushed my cheek as he brought his lips to mine. We basked in the moment, savoring every second. I'd thought I had been complete when he'd come into my life but the little life that he'd planted inside of me had filled me to capacity. I was overflowing with joy and gratitude.

"I love you, too." I whispered back on the verge of tears. "Happy New Year *and* Happy Anniversary, baby."

GREY HUFFINGTON

. . .

THE END...

HUFFINGTON NEWS

Join over 8,000 honorary Huffington residents for monthly broadcasts delivered right to their preferred devices.

Broadcasts include but aren't limited to:

- A beautiful monthly newsletter detailing everything happening in Huffington
- Extensive snippets of upcoming projects (sneak peeks)
- Release day reminders that include links (to remove the guest work from searching for books on Amazon/Ghuffington.com)
- First to hear about surprise releases
- Exclusive discounts + offers for Huffington residents
- A monthly wrap-up detailing everything that has happened in Huffington since the release of the Huffington Newsletter

GHUFFINGTON.COM

Ready to become a resident?
Click here.
[https://huffingtonnews.ck.page/4693a79283]

MORE FROM GREY HUFFINGTON

Find the entire collection of Grey Huffington titles below. Titles in the catalog are available in eBook (amazon.com, + ghuffington.com), paperback (ghuffington.com), or audiobook (audible + ghuffington.com) formats.

Syx + the City
Syx + the City 2
Syx Thirty Seven
Syxth Giving
Syx Whole Weeks

Wilde + Reckless
Wilde + Relentless
Wilde + Restless

Mr. Intentional
Unearth Me

MORE FROM GREY HUFFINGTON

The Sweetest Revenge
The Sweetest Redemption

Half + Half
The Emancipation of Emoree

Sleigh
Sleigh Squared

The Gifted
Memo
Give her Love. Give her Flowers.

Unbreak Me
Uncover Me

As we Learn
As we Love

Just Wanna Mean the Most to You
Sensitivity
10,000 Hours
Darke Hearts
muse.

Softly
Peace + Quiet
Press Rewind
Jagged Edges
My Person
The Realm of Riot Thimble

MORE FROM GREY HUFFINGTON

Whose Love Story is it Anyway?
Unhand Me

Home*
Blues*
31st*
Now That We're Here.*

Then Let's Fuck About It*
Giving Thanks

A Month of Sundays Ep 1
A Month of Sundays Ep 2
A Month of Sundays Ep 3
Dinner at Ever + Luca's
Saylah
The Mayor's Ball
Elm

THE EISENBERG EFFECT
Luca
Lyric
Ever*
Laike
Baisleigh*
Liam

THE DOMINO EFFECT
Ledge
Halo*
Lawe

MORE FROM GREY HUFFINGTON

Kleuless*

BERKELEY BRED
Malachi
Anna*
Milo
Makai
Glacier*
Mercer
Vallei*

THE GREY LIST
Chemistry "The Chemist"
Egypt
Rather "The Therapist"

--

* signifies the publication is available EXCLUSIVELY on ghuffington.com.

--

Prefer Audiobooks?

Did you know **there's a library FULL of audiobooks on ghuffington.com** for the lovers who listen?

We're building so you can continue to listen to the books you've been hearing good things about. There are currently over 17 audiobooks waiting for you to indulge.

In addition to our audiobook library, we have an audiobook club for those who care to save 40-50% off their audiobooks. **Heard is not mandatory to shop audiobooks but we do recommend taking a look at the perks.**

Audiobooks Available (**exclusively on GHuffington.com**)

Chemistry
Egypt
Ever
Baisleigh
Halo
Kleuless
Anna
Glacier
Vallei (coming soon)
Muse.
Elm.
Sensitivity
The Realm of Riot Thimble
Whose Love Story is it Anyway?
Unhand Me